Hello Cooper,
I hope you like the story in this, there are some pages in the back for you to draw some pictures of Simon and his friends!
Merry Christmas 2023!!

With love from your great grandma Nana Cou

MY NAME IS SIMON
I AM A SNAIL

Melanie Richardson Dundy

MDCT Publishing
mdctpublishng@gmail.com
melanie.dundy@icloud.com
Website: ChildrensBooksByMelanie.com

There are others all around me,
as you can clearly see.
But they just glance as they pass by.
They don't care about me.

I know I look quite different.
I do not quite fit in.
I only slide along the sand
while they all swiftly swim.

Behind my back, they talk and joke
because I cannot float.
I bet they too would sink real fast
if they had shells to tote.

But I can do things they cannot.
They should just watch and see.
I can attach and hold on tight
to boats and rocks at sea.

If danger tries to seek them out,
they all scurry and hide.
I have my shell to keep me safe.
I just twist up inside.

I wish I was purple or red,
or maybe orange and blue.
I wish I could swim really fast,
rather than slide on goo.

It's true I have but one real foot,
but why do they make fun?
It is quite clear from where I sit,
they all indeed have none.

I was happy to have my friend.
We talked and played all day.
Toby was great, and I was thrilled,
to play and play and play.

He whipped right through the ocean waves —
swam to the water's top.
Moving at turtle, breakneck speed,
I thought my shell would pop.

I'd never been this high before.
There was so much to see.
I never thought or even dreamt
this could happen to me.

I was giddy to have a friend;
was happy as could be.
I did not want this day to end —
it was magic for me.

CPSIA information can be obtained
at www.ICGtesting.com
Printed in the USA
BVHW061655190922
647374BV00001B/4